HAROLD *and the*
PURPLE CRAYON

HAROLD
and the
PURPLE CRAYON

by
Crockett Johnson

HarperCollins*Publishers*

Library of Congress catalog card number: 55–7683
ISBN: 0–06–022935–7
ISBN: 0–06–022936–5 (lib. bdg.)
ISBN: 0–06–443022–7 (pbk.)
14 15 16 17 SCP 50 49 48 47 46 45 44 43

One evening, after thinking it over for some time, Harold decided to go for a walk in the moonlight.

There wasn't any moon, and Harold needed a
moon for a walk in the moonlight.

And he needed something to walk on.

He made a long straight path so he wouldn't
get lost.

And he set off on his walk, taking his big
purple crayon with him.

But he didn't seem to be getting anywhere
on the long straight path.

So he left the path for a short cut across
a field. And the moon went with him.

The short cut led right to where Harold
thought a forest ought to be.

He didn't want to get lost in the woods.
So he made a very small forest, with just
one tree in it.

It turned out to be an apple tree.

The apples would be very tasty, Harold thought, when they got red.

So he put a frightening dragon under the tree to guard the apples.

It was a terribly frightening dragon.

It even frightened Harold. He backed away.

His hand holding the purple crayon shook.

Suddenly he realized what was happening.

But by then Harold was over his head in
an ocean.

He came up thinking fast.

And in no time he was climbing aboard a
trim little boat.

He quickly set sail.

And the moon sailed along with him.

After he had sailed long enough, Harold
made land without much trouble.

He stepped ashore on the beach, wondering where he was.

The sandy beach reminded Harold of picnics.
And the thought of picnics made him hungry.

So he laid out a nice simple picnic lunch.

There was nothing but pie.

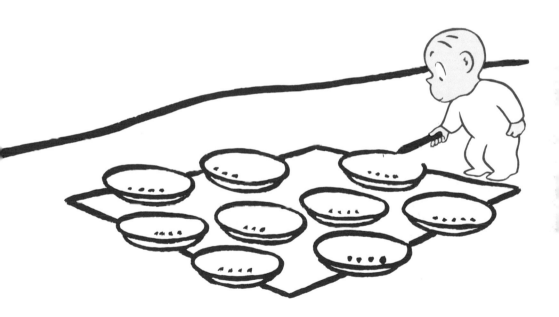

But there were all nine kinds of pie that
Harold liked best.

When Harold finished his picnic there was
quite a lot left.

He hated to see so much delicious pie go
to waste.

So Harold left a very hungry moose and a deserving porcupine to finish it up.

And, off he went, looking for a hill to
climb, to see where he was.

Harold knew that the higher up he went,
the farther he could see. So he decided
to make the hill into a mountain.

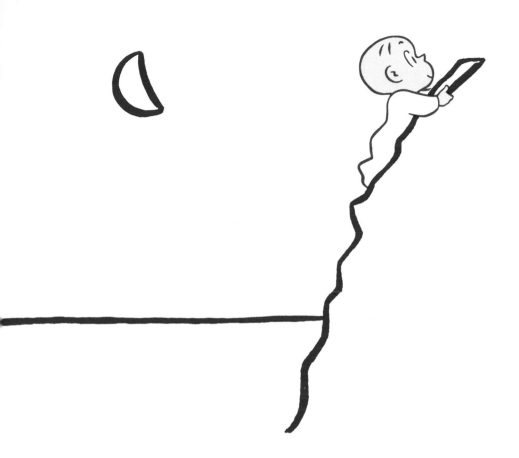

If he went high enough, he thought, he could see the window of his bedroom.

He was tired and he felt he ought to be
getting to bed.

He hoped he could see his bedroom window
from the top of the mountain.

But as he looked down over the other side
he slipped—

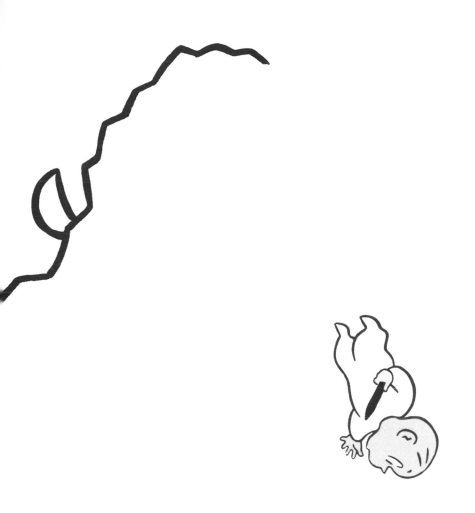

And there wasn't any other side of the
mountain. He was falling, in thin air.

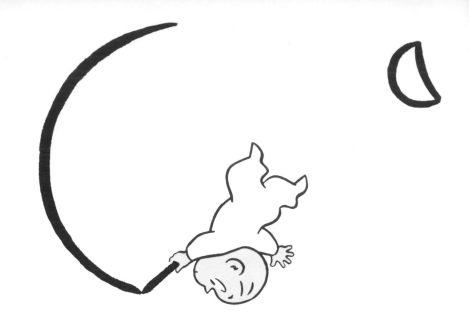

But, luckily, he kept his wits and his
purple crayon.

He made a balloon and he grabbed on to it.

And he made a basket under the balloon big
enough to stand in.

He had a fine view from the balloon but he
couldn't see his window. He couldn't even
see a house.

So he made a house, with windows.

And he landed the balloon on the grass in the front yard.

None of the windows was his window.

He tried to think where his window ought
to be.

He made some more windows.

He made a big building full of windows.

He made lots of buildings full of windows.

He made a whole city full of windows.

But none of the windows was his window.

He couldn't think where it might be.

He decided to ask a policeman.

The policeman pointed the way Harold was going anyway. But Harold thanked him.

And he walked along with the moon,
wishing he was in his room and in bed.

Then, suddenly, Harold remembered.

He remembered where his bedroom window
was, when there was a moon.

It was always right around the moon.

And then Harold made his bed.